INVESTED

Cleo Kaine

Invested is a work of fiction. It is not meant to depict, portray, or represent any particular person, living or dead, actual events, establishment or organization. Other characters, places, and events are products of the author's imagination and are used fictitiously to give the book a sense of reality and authenticity. Any resemblance of fictionalized events or incidents that involve a real person is purely coincidental.

J K Media
P O Box 1986
Pine Bluff, AR 71613

Book cover was made by Dynasty Cover Design

ISBN: 979-8-9987427-0-5

Dedication

I would like to dedicate this book to my family who encourage me to continue to write my stories. I would like to thank my TRIBE (Fans). For without you all I would not be writing these stories. I would like to thank Renna Garnette and Erica Reams for pushing me to do this. Even when I didn't feel like writing, you all would tell me to write any. God will give you the words to type. I also would like to thank my best friend from the Chi, Sage Ofir. I appreciate you listening to all my stories. Finally, I would like to thank God, for without him, I wouldn't be able to share my stories to you.

Chapter 1

Today was a day that Aketa Collins had been planning for months. She pulled out all the tricks for tonight. She had the champagne chilling in the silver and black bucket, and the long flute glasses were sitting on the side of the bucket. Her dinner table was typically set for four, but tonight was set for two. She had the red candles lit to create the mood. She put out her crystal vase that Ellis Allan, her man, got her for their fifth anniversary. He buys her roses every year. It is usually a rose every year. He will bring home fifteen roses this year, for today marks the beginning of their fifteenth year together.

Their daughters weren't there that night. She had sent them over to her mother's house. Her mother keeps them occasionally so they can have some time alone. She always said that it was good for the relationship. Ellis and Aketa have been in this relationship since their sophomore year of college. Out of all these years, Aketa earned her bachelor's in English and a master's in mass communication. Then, she decides to take it a step further. She went to law school and earned her JD. Ellis went on to earn his bachelor's in psychology. Afterward, he went into the police academy. It was something that he always wanted to do.

This relationship has been going on for fifteen years. In recent years, they have managed to start a family. They have two lovely daughters, Elisha and Akera. They moved out of their one-bedroom apartment into a townhouse uptown. They worked hard to get to where they are now. Aketa has one problem she has been battling with Ellis for years.   He refuses to marry her.
Despite her mother's disapproval, Aketa had chosen her own path, believing that Ellis would eventually propose. For now, she was content. She was with a man as wonderful as Ellis Allan, and she clung to the hope that one day, he would be ready to take the next step.

Ellis came in at around about seven, as he does every night. He swung open the door, pulled off his black coat, and hung it on the coat rack at the entrance. Aketa was expecting him to be carrying some roses in his arms. He walks past Aketa, not noticing what she is wearing. She wore his favorite red dress, which he loved seeing her in. He walked right past the dining room, not noticing the dinner she prepared for him. Ellis went to the bedroom. Aketa walked into the room while Ellis was stripping out of his work clothes. He pulled out his jeans and football jersey when Aketa coughed to get his attention. He looked over at her with his hazel eyes. He had noticed her, but the disappointment in Aketa's eyes was unmistakable.

"Is tonight date night?" he asked.

Aketa looked at him with evil eyes and said, "You seriously don't know what tonight is."

Ellis thought about it. He knew he had forgotten something. Ellis should have gone to the flower shop and picked up the roses. He forgot after all these years.

"Sorry, Keta," he said. "I forgot what today is."

"Well," Aketa said. "Get dressed, and let's eat."

Ellis had made other plans. His best friend, Jeremy, had tickets for tonight's Tigers football game, and he wasn't willing to give up his fifty-yard line seat.

"Keta," he said, "Jeremy and I are going to the game tonight. Can we do this another night?"

"Another night?" Aketa said.

"I promise I will make it up to you," he said.

Ellis gave her the look he usually gives her when he wants something. She typically gives in with this look. He took one look at her and knew that she was hurt.

"I promise I will make it up to you, baby," he said.

He kissed her on the forehead and continued to get dressed. The doorbell rang. Aketa went to answer it. A six-foot bald caramel man stood at the door. He looks fit for a man in his thirties. He was wearing his Tigers football jersey. It was Jeremy.

"Hello, beautiful," Jeremy said with a big smile. Ellis walked into the room. He saw how Jeremy was looking at Aketa.

"Man," Jeremy said, "if you weren't my best friend, I would take Aketa from you."

They both laughed. Ellis kissed Aketa. She was angry at Ellis. She couldn't believe he had forgotten the one day they had been celebrating for the last fifteen years.

"I will see you later tonight, Baby," he said to her as he grabbed his coat and walked out the door.

Aketa went to the dining room and started to clean up.

Later on that night, Aketa was in bed. Ellis came home. He was toasted. He had been drinking with Jeremy most of that night. He went to the room that he shared with Aketa. He pulled off all his clothes and got on the bed with her. He started to rub against her to try to wake her up. She just moved closer to the edge of their queen-sized bed. He hurried over and went undercover. He started to remove her panties. Aketa jumped up as he was pulling them.

"You expected me to give you some after what you did tonight," Aketa snarled.

"What did I do?" he asked stupidly.

"Really?" she said. "You forgot our anniversary, and you expect to come in here drunk and think that everything is alright."

Aketa grabbed her favorite pillow and some covers.

"Where are you going?" Ellis asked.

"Away from you," she answered.

Aketa left the room and went to her oldest daughter's room, who wasn't there. She closed and locked the door. Ellis came behind her and knocked on the door, but Aketa didn't answer. She knew that if she ignored him, he would go to bed and leave her alone.

"I am sorry, Keta," he shouted.

Aketa still ignored him. Ellis then went to the room and went to sleep. He will talk to her in the morning about it.

Chapter 2

In Ellis and Aketa's household, they had a routine. Ellis gets up at 5 a.m. and does his daily exercises. Aketa gets up about thirty minutes later. She gets the girls up and helps them get ready for school. Ellis comes back about forty minutes later. By this time, Aketa is cooking breakfast. Ellis goes to the bathroom and gets ready for work. She feeds the girls and walks them to the bus stop. When Aketa returns from taking the girls to the bus stop, Ellis is usually eating breakfast at the kitchen table. At this time, she goes to get ready for work. When she returned to the kitchen, Ellis was about to leave. He goes over and kisses her before he tells her he loves her. Lately, however, the love has slowly started to fade away.

When Aketa got to her office today, the first person she saw was her administrative assistant, Diana. When Aketa walked in, Diana talked on the phone as she does every morning. Usually, she is on the phone with a relative or a friend she met just the other day. Diana hurried up and rushed off the phone.

"Good morning, Ms. Collins," Diana said.

"Good morning," Aketa said.

She walked into her office, hung up her coat, and put her briefcase on her desk. When she sat at the desk, she opened the briefcase and took out the papers she had been working on at home. She then sat down behind her desk and started to read them.

It was lunchtime. Aketa was still working when a tall, slender, chocolate woman entered her office. She wore an indigo blue pencil dress with heels to match. Phaedra Williams has been Aketa's best friend since they were kids. Phaedra works as a stylist for celebrities. Phaedra usually comes in at lunchtime, and they go out to lunch. During their lunchtime, they typically have their ordinary girl talk. She saw Aketa with her head buried into a brief. Phaedra coughed to get her attention. Aketa did not look up. Phaedra knew something was wrong because Aketa only buried herself in her work when she was upset. Phaedra approached her desk and grabbed the brief from Aketa's hand.

"What's wrong with you?" Phaedra asked.

"Nothing," Aketa answered.

"Well," Phaedra said, "It is time for lunch."

Aketa picked up the phone and asked Diana to order Chinese for them. Phaedra sat on the red leather couch in Aketa's office.

"How was anniversary night?" Phaedra asked.

"None existence," Aketa replied.

"Now that is what is wrong with you," Phaedra said. "Ellis is an asshole."

"He decided to spend our anniversary with Jeremy."

"Oh no, he didn't," Phaedra said.

"He said that he had forgotten and would make it up to me," Aketa said.

"Girl," Phaedra said, "you know he will not do it."

"He will," Aketa said.

"Keta," Phaedra said, "he hasn't married you all this time. He is not going to marry you."

Diana walked in with lunch. She sat it down on the coffee table, then sat on the couch with Phaedra.

"What did I miss?" Diana asked.

"Nothing," Aketa answered.

"Umm, no," Phaedra said. "Her anniversary night wasn't all that."

"No wonder she came in so grumpy today," Diana said.

Aketa raised her voice and said, "I wasn't grumpy this morning!"

"Yes, you were," Diana said. "You didn't come out for your usual cup of joe."

"Now, you have been drinking coffee since I have known you," Phaedra said.

"There is nothing wrong," said Aketa.

"You know he will never marry you," Diana said.

"I said the same thing, too," Phaedra said.

"Why are you both doubting that he will ever ask me to marry him?" Aketa asked.

"If he hasn't asked in all these years," Phaedra said. "He is not going to ask. Plus, you and he have already started a family. I told you should have married him while pregnant with Elisha."

Aketa knew that Phaedra had a point. She has been wanting to get married for a long time. Ellis always came up with some flimsy excuse for why they couldn't get married. The closest they ever came to getting married was two years ago. Ellis called it off. He said something didn't feel right about it.

"I would have left him after the fourth year," Diana said. "I couldn't be with a man like Ellis."

"Why don't you ask him why he won't marry you," Phaedra said. "Inquiring minds would like to know."

They ate their lunch. Aketa thought about what Phaedra said. She felt that it was time for her to give Ellis an ultimatum. Tonight, she was going to see what he was going to say.

After work, Aketa went to pick up the girls from after-school care. She went home. She helped the girls with their homework. After she finished helping, she started dinner. The girls were in their room watching television. Ellis came home. He walked into the kitchen where Aketa was cooking dinner.

"Hi, Baby," he said.

He walked over to her and kissed her as he usually does.

"We need to talk," Aketa told him.

"What about?" he asked.

"Well," she said, "I have been thinking. We have been together for fifteen years. We need to get married."

"Why do we need to have this discussion again?" he asked.

"Do you want to do right in God's eyes?" Aketa asked.

"We are doing right in God's eyes. We have two beautiful girls that we are raising together. We have a townhouse together. What more do you want?"

"But we are living in sin," Aketa replied.

"We are married already," Ellis said.

"Not legally," Aketa said. "If anything happens to you, we don't get anything. Your family gets it all."

"Like I said," Ellis said. "I'll marry you when God tells me to. And so far, God hasn't told me to marry you."

"So, God hasn't moved you to marry me," Aketa said.

"By the way," he said, "when did you get all religious on me?"

Aketa didn't say a word. She had made up her mind. God moved her to do something. Leave Ellis Allan.

Chapter 3

Aketa sat in bed the following day. She didn't get any sleep last night. She stayed up on the computer looking for a house. She plans to take off today and go to the bank to see if she can get pre-approved for a loan so that she can know how much she works with.

Ellis got up late. He didn't go for his morning jog as he does every morning. Instead, Ellis went straight to the shower and got ready for work. He also noticed no breakfast was fixed as it typically is every morning. Ellis grabs a bowl and a box of cereal. He poured himself a bowl. The girls came into the kitchen. They did not see their mother. They were also used to having breakfast before they went to school.

"Where is Mama?" Elisha asked.

Ellis looked at his oldest daughter and said, "She is still in bed."

Then Ellis walked over to the cabinet and took out two more bowls for the girls. He gave them the bowls, and they poured their cereal into them.

"Daddy," the youngest one, Akera, said, "can you take us to school?"

Akera looks just like her mother, but she has his eyes. He never could say no to her.

"Sure," he said.

When they finished eating, he put the bowls in the dishwasher. They all went to his truck, and he took the girls to school.

When Aketa heard the door close, she got up. She went to the bathroom to get ready to go to the bank. She looked at herself in the mirror and saw her bloodshot red eyes. She had been crying because Ellis had disappointed her. She had to get it together. Aketa hopped into the shower. She got herself ready to do this.

When she got to the bank, she went to the loan department and walked up to the desk. A large, tan woman with glasses was sitting on the other side of the desk.

"May I help you?" the woman asked.

"I would like to apply for a loan for a house," Aketa answered.

"Have you talked to an agent?" she asked.

"No," Aketa replied.

"Do you have an account with us?" the woman asked.

"Yes," Aketa replied. She went into her brown purse and gave the woman her account card. The woman looked it up. Her eyes widened as she saw the amount in the account. She handed her an application.

"You need to fill this out," she said as she handed her the application and her card back.

"Thank you," Aketa said.

She sat down and started filling out the application. When Aketa was finished, she handed the application to the woman. She told Aketa to have a seat and that someone would be with her in a minute. About five minutes later, another lady exited the office behind the desk. She was an olive-skinned woman with long, slender legs. She went to the desk and acquired Aketa's application. She reviewed it before she called Aketa to her office. She was impressed.

"Aketa Collins," she called her name.

Aketa pulled up from the seat that she was sitting in. She walked toward the lady. The lady escorted Aketa to her office. She opens the door, and Aketa walks in. The lady walks in behind her.

"My name is Karlie Lane," the lady said as she reached out to shake Aketa's hand.

"I am Aketa Collins," she said.

They both sat down. Karlie entered the information from the application onto the computer. When she was finished, she smiled.

"Ms. Collin," Karlie said, "I have good news for you. You have been pre-approved for $250,000. All you have to do now is shop around. Come back when you find what you want, and we will complete the paperwork.

Aketa smiled. She was so happy. Karlie handed her some papers to sign. She made a copy and gave it to Aketa. Aketa got up to get ready to leave.

"Good luck in your house hunting," Karlie said.

"Thank you, Ms. Lane," Aketa said.

She left the bank. She drove through a few neighborhoods she wouldn't mind staying in. She wrote the address so a real estate agent could check it out. Later that evening, she called an agent and started making appointments to look at houses. In two weeks, she found a home with which she fell in love. She went to the bank. She filled out the extra paperwork. She was approved but couldn't move in until the house exited escrow. Now that she had to put a plan into play, it was time to move.

While the house was in escrow, Aketa started shopping for furniture. She didn't want to carry anything from the townhouse except their clothes. She bought a brown leather living room set and a lovely dinette table. One weekend, she decided to take the girls shopping. She let them pick out their bedroom sets with comforters and curtains to match. When they returned home, Ellis played his football game on the PlayStation in the living room.

"Daddy," Akera said, "Mama bought us new bedroom sets."

"Oh, she did," Ellis said.

"It was time for a new bed anyway," Aketa said, looking at Akera like she was in trouble.

Akera is a daddy's girl. She can't hold water. She is always telling him something. One year, Akera told Ellis about his surprise birthday party.

"Go put up what we bought," Aketa told the girls.

They both went into their rooms. Ellis was still sitting in his favorite black lounger playing the game. Aketa went to the kitchen to prepare dinner. Ellis got up and went into the kitchen.

"Did you buy us a new bed, too," Ellis said, being sarcastic.

Aketa looked at him and said, "No, I didn't."

"And why not?" he asked.

"Did we just get a new bed?" Aketa asked.

Ellis couldn't say another word. He sat down at the table and picked up the newspaper.

"The boys and I are attending a football game in Texas next month. We are going to be gone for a week."

"Ok," Aketa said.

"Will you and the girls be alright?" Ellis asked.

"Yes," she replied.

Typically, Aketa makes a big fuss about him going to the football game without her and the girls. But this gave her the perfect opportunity to move out. The house should be out of escrow a week before he leaves. She didn't care about going this year.

Three weeks later, the house came out of escrow. The agent delivered the keys to her office. Aketa was so happy. She went home early that day to the new house on Vermont Drive. She walks through the four-bedroom and two-and-a-half-bath house. She was ready to move in. She went to the utilities and had them cut on. She went to her mother's house and told her about her new house. Her mother thought that she was kidding. But Aketa took her to the house. Her mother loved it. That weekend, Aketa, her mother, Diana, and Phaedra cleaned the house. The furniture came on Monday. Phaedra and Aketa went shopping for household appliances and groceries. By Friday, she was ready to move in.

Ellis got up and prepared for his boys' trip on Saturday morning. He had his bags by the door, waiting for Jeremy to pick him up. Aketa rose early as usual. She went downstairs to see him off. She fixed herself a cup of coffee and sat in the den, waiting for him to leave. She usually didn't do this. Ellis didn't notice that it was something different this time. He was too pumped about going to Texas. He was looking out the window like a kid. When Jeremy finally pulled up, he grabbed his bags.

"I'll see you later, baby," he said.

Aketa waved at him. He walked over to her and kissed her on the forehead. She continued to sip her coffee as Ellis walked out the door. Aketa got up. She put her cup on the coffee table and looked out the window. When she saw him pull off, she called Phaedra to help her move.

It took Phaedra about an hour to come over. She was dressed to move, and she brought Diana with her. They started by packing Aketa's closet, which they put in Phaedra's truck. Elisha woke up and went to the kitchen; she saw what they were doing.

"Mama," Elisha said, "what are you doing?"

"We are moving today," Aketa replied.

"Where?" Elisha asked.

"Into a house," Aketa answered. "Can you get some of those boxes and pack up your room?"

"Ok," Elisha answered.

Elisha picked up a few boxes and went to her room, smiling. Aketa continued to pack up her closet when she heard Akera getting up.

"Elisha," Aketa said, "keep your sister busy until we finish. Better yet, get dressed. We are going to eat brunch."

Elisha put the boxes down and did what her mother asked. They rushed to put all the boxes into the truck. Phaedra and Diana left just when Elisha and Akera came into the room.

"We are ready," Akera said.

"Go get in the car," Aketa said.

They got into the car and ate brunch. When they were finished, Aketa took them to her mother's house. Elisha wanted to go to a friend instead, so she took over there until she finished moving everything.

Aketa met back up with Phaedra and Diana at the house. They were unloading the truck.

"I think it would be better if we got a U-Haul and made one trip," Diana suggested.

"I guess we could get a U-Haul," Aketa said.

They went to get a U-Haul. Once they rented it, they returned to the townhouse and packed everything else they were taking out of the house. They finished around about five that evening. Diana drove the truck to the house, and they unpacked it. They flopped down on the couch after everything was out of the truck. They were tired.

"I didn't realize moving was so much work," Phaedra said.

"I am hiring a moving company when I move," Diana said.

They all laughed and rested on the couch. At around seven, Aketa went to get the girls to bring them to their new house. She went and picked up Elisha first. Then, she went to pick up Akera and her mother. They all went to the house. The girl's eyes widened as they approached this big reddish-brown house on Vermont Drive.

"Mama," Akera said, "whose house is this?"

"It's ours," Aketa replied.

"Is Daddy staying with us?" Akera asked.

Aketa smiled and said, "No."

This upsets Akera. When they entered the house, Akera forgot about her dad and was ready to enter her room. Diana and Phaedra were in the kitchen looking for the plates. They had ordered pizza. The girls ran to the kitchen and got a plate.

"How do you like the place so far?" Her mom asked the girls.

"I love it, Granny," Elisha said.

Akera frowned. She wanted to be with her dad.

"Well," Phaedra said, "your rooms are upstairs."

That put a smile on Akera's face, and they ran upstairs and saw their names on the doors of their room. They open the door to see the furniture that they had picked out. It was nice. Once the girls were in bed, Phaedra took Aketa's mom back to the house. Phaedra came back, and they drank red wine.

"I wonder how Ellis will act after discovering you move?" Diana inquired.

"I don't know," Aketa answered. "And I don't care."

They continue to drink their wine.

Ellis came back from his trip a day earlier than he expected. He saw his truck in the driveway but didn't see Aketa's car. Ordinarily, Aketa is at home by now. He went into the house and dropped his bags at the kitchen door. He saw a piece of paper on the counter. He picked it up and read it. It said:

Dear Ellis,

I can no longer live like this anymore. We have been together for fifteen years, and you refuse to marry me. So,

I decided to leave you. I want to get married one day. Something that you don't want to do. I wish you well in life.

Love,

Aketa

He pulled out his phone and called Aketa. She didn't answer her phone. He called again. It went straight to voicemail. So, he called her mother. She didn't answer the phone. He ran to the room. He looked in the closet and saw all her clothes gone. He went to the girls' room and saw everything gone.

Ellis decided right then and there that he would find her.

Chapter 4

After winning the Dumont Case, the company
wanted to treat Claire, who is her colleague, and Aketa to
dinner at Monroe's. They had a tab with this restaurant.
Mr. Dumont called and told the restaurant they could have
anything on the menu. Before they went to the restaurant,
they went back to the office.

When Aketa returned, she saw Ellis sitting in front
of Diana's desk. She walked past him like she didn't notice
he was there. Ellis got up and walked into the office
behind her. Aketa sat behind her desk. Ellis sat on the
couch.

"What do you want?" Aketa asked him.

"Why did you move out?" Ellis asked.

"Did you get my letter?" she asked him.

"Yes," he replied. "When are you coming back
home?"

Ellis looked at her thoughtfully. Life as he became
accustomed to had been disrupted. He only wanted Aketa
and the girls to come home with him.

"I will go to my house when I get off work," Aketa
said.

"Where do you live now?" Ellis asked.

"You are a detective," Aketa said sarcastically. "You'll figure it out."

The phone rang. It was Diana. She was reminding her about a meeting with Claire that she had in ten minutes.

"I have a meeting in ten minutes," Aketa told Ellis. "Is there anything else that you would like to know?"

"When can I see my girls?" Ellis asked.

"I'll make arrangements with you later," she said.

Ellis got up off the couch. He walked out. Diana came into the office.

"So," Diana said, "what happened?"

"He wants me to come home," Aketa said. "I told him that I already had a home."

"What else?" Diana asked.

"Nothing," she replied. "I need you to call Phaedra and tell her to meet us at Monroe's restaurant tonight."

"Monroe's?" Diana inquired.

"Yes, Monroe's," Aketa said.

Diana went back to her desk to do what Aketa asked of her. Aketa went to her private bathroom and freshened herself up. She called her mother and said she would be late picking up the girls. She grabbed her purse and walked out of the office. Claire had just walked up.

"Are you ready?" she asked.

"Yes," Aketa replied. "I asked Diana and Phaedra to join us."

"I don't mind," Claire said.

They each decide to drive their vehicles because they can go home after dinner. They met up at Monroe's. Phaedra was in her car checking her make-up. Aketa got out of her car and tapped on Phaedra's window. Phaedra jumped. She rolled down her window.

"Don't scare me like that!" she roared at Aketa.

Aketa laughed. Phaedra rolled up her window and got out of the car. By the time they got to the restaurant doors, Diana and Claire had come up.

Diana and Claire greeted Phaedra. They all walked in together. A tall, muscular-built, yellow man greeted them.

"Welcome to Monroe's," he said in his Creole accent. "Do you have reservations with us tonight?"

"Yes, Dumont," Claire answered.

The man looked down at the book and saw the name.

"So, you are the attorneys that won Mr. Dumont's case," he said. "Follow me."

He escorted them to a table in the restaurant's center, where they all sat down. He then handed them a menu.

"Mr. Dumont said order anything and everything your heart desires," the Creole man said. "Your garçon will be with you shortly."

"Thank you," Aketa said.

The man walked off. The ladies looked at the menu. They discussed among themselves what they were going to order. A young man came over. They asked for a bottle of red wine. He took their order when he returned with the bottle and four wine glasses. They talked among themselves until their food arrived. They ate their food while laughing and talking. They had such a good time. When they were finished, they ordered dessert. Before the desert came out, a medium-height bronze man walked out of the kitchen. His hair was low cut, and his beard was nicely trimmed. He wore a white jacket that was partially open. You can see his blue T-shirt under it. His pants and shoes were black. He walked over to every table to ask if they enjoyed their meal. He approached Aketa's table and couldn't stop staring at her. He froze for a minute.

"Hello," he said. "I am Chef Jesse Monroe. Are you young ladies enjoying your meal?"

They all nodded their heads yes.

"It was very delicious," Aketa said.

Jesse smiled. Now he had a voice to put with this beautiful person. The host came over.

"These are the attorneys that won Mr. Dumont's case," the host said.

"I have attorneys in my establishment tonight," Jessie said, smiling.

"Yes, yes you do," Claire said. "Will you excuse me while I go to the restroom?"

She excused herself to the restroom. Jesse took her seat next to Aketa.

"Do you have a card," Jesse asked Aketa.

She reached into her LV purse to get a business card. She pulled out the card, which she gave to him. Jesse put it in his jacket pocket.

He got up as Claire was coming back to her seat.

He looked at Aketa and said, "You will hear from me soon."

He walked back to the kitchen.

The following day, Aketa came to work with a smile on her face. She walked in, almost skipping into her office. Diana noticed her big grin.

"Why are we so happy this morning?" Diana asked.

Aketa stopped at her desk and said, "For no reason."

She went into the office and sat behind her desk. As she was about to start her work for the day, there was a knock on the door.

"Come in," she said in her sweet voice.

To her surprise, Jesse walks in with a tray and coffee. Her smile got bigger.

"Good morning," he said. "I decided to fix some breakfast for you this morning."

He sat the tray on her desk. She opened it and saw creole eggs benedict with beignets.

"Thank you," she said to him.

"You're welcome," he said.

Jesse sat down on the couch. Her smile became even more extensive. She could not believe he was there at her office.

"What do I owe the honor of you coming with breakfast this morning?" she asked.

"I wanted to see you again," he answered.

By this time, Aketa was blushing.

"And I want to ask you for a date this Friday."

"I have to check my calendar to see if I am available," Aketa replied. She looked at her calendar. "What time?"

"Seven," he said. "I will pick you up at your office after work."

"Where are we going?" Aketa asked. "To your restaurant?"

"No," Jesse said. "I have a special place in mind."

"Ok," she said.

He rose off the couch. He said, "I see you at seven on Friday."

Aketa smiled as he walked out the door. He didn't know it but had just made it Aketa's day.

Chapter 5

It was late Friday evening. Aketa was working in her office when Diana entered and sat on the couch. Aketa didn't notice that Diana was there; her head was buried in her work. Diana just sat there and watched Aketa as she worked. Twenty minutes later, Aketa finally looked up and saw Diana sitting there. She put down what she was working on.

"Do you know it is past time to go?" Diana inquired.

"What time is it?" Aketa asked.

"Almost seven," Diana replied.

Aketa realized that she didn't have time to go to the house and change. She jumped up out of her seat and ran into her office bathroom. She had a little black dress in her office in case she wanted to go out with her friends right after work. She washed herself off and put on a fresh pair of panties. She wasn't going to give him any on the first date. Still, she wanted to be fresh. She walked out of the bathroom wearing her black dress and three-inch black pumps. Jesse was sitting on the couch talking to Diana. They were both laughing and talking.

"Hum," Aketa coughed.

They both looked up and saw Aketa standing in her little black dress. She had her hair down. She had a little clutch to match. Jesse got up, grabbed her hand, and kissed it. Aketa blushed.

"You look beautiful," Jesse said.

"Thank you," Aketa said.

"Are you ready to go?" he asked.

"Where are y'all going?" Diana asked.

Jesse smiled and replied, "It is a surprise."

"Oh," Aketa said. "I will see you later, Diana."

Jesse and Aketa walked out the door. They got onto the elevator that went to the parking garage. He escorted her to his black Dodge charger. He opens the passenger door for her. He helps Aketa in the car. He went to the other side and got in. He started the car and drove off.

"Are we going to your restaurant?" Aketa asked.

Jesse smiled and replied, "No."

The rest of the drive was quiet. Jesse turned into a parking lot of a building that looked like a warehouse. He parked the car near the door. Jesse got out of the vehicle. He walked over to the passenger side and opened the door for Aketa. Jesse helped her out of the car. He escorted her to the front door of the building. A young man stood at the door with a black jacket, blue t-shirt, and jeans. He saw Jesse and greeted him.

"Good evening, Mr. Monroe," the young man said. "Mr. Undre has your table waiting for you."

The young man opens the door of the building. Aketa thought she would see an empty room with one table. She was shocked to see that it was a club. It wasn't bad looking. It was a colossal-sized dance floor and a DJ booth. There was no one in the club. It was a table set up in the middle of the dance floor. It had a bouquet of roses sitting on it. It was set very nicely. Jesse escorted Aketa over to the table. He pulled out her chair for her. Aketa sat down, and Jesse helped her push her to the table. Then he sat down in his seat. A waiter came over to them. He had a bottle of wine.

"May I interest you in a bottle of Pinot noir?" he asked.

"Yes," Jesse answered.

The waiter poured the wine into the glass for them. He walks off to the back.

"Did you cook before you came to get me?" Aketa asked.

"No," he said, "I have a friend that owes me a favor."

Aketa smiled. Jesse was happy that he made her smile.

"You have a beautiful smile," he said.

"Thank you," she said. "Tell me about yourself."

"Well," he said, "I am the oldest of two kids. I have a younger sister named Jamie. I went to culinary school in New York."

"You must love to cook," Aketa said.

"Yes," he replied, "I do. When I was little, I used to help my grandmother cook. She taught me everything that I know."

Aketa took a sip of wine. She listens to Jesse talk about cooking. You could see that he has a passion for cooking. A few minutes into the conversation, their appetizer was served. They continued to talk as they ate. When dinner was served, their conversation came to a cease. Aketa hated to speak while eating. After they finish, they continue the conversation.

"What is your story?" Jesse asked.

Aketa didn't want to tell him that she had just ended a relationship of fifteen years with her baby daddy. She didn't want to tell him she had two girls that she was raising by herself. She didn't know what to tell him.

"I am an attorney trying to make a living," she replied.

"Did you always want to be an attorney?" he asked.

"Yes," Aketa answered.

"Where did you come from?"

"I am from Butler, but I live in Rosewood," she replied.

"That is a nice neighborhood," Jesse said. "I started to buy a house out there, but I settled for a house in Butler."

When their dessert was brought to the table, Aketa put her napkin in her lap and began to eat. They talked and laughed as they ate. After dessert, they danced on the dance floor. It was only the two of them.

Around about three o'clock that morning, Jesse took her back to her office. She was wearing his jacket. He walked Aketa to her car.

"Thank you for the nice dinner," Aketa said with a smile.

"You are welcome," Jesse said. "I hope it won't be our last dinner together."

Aketa smiled and said, "I hope not to."

As Aketa was about to open the door to her car, she turned around to tell Jesse goodbye, but Jesse kissed her. She was going to push him away, but his lips were so soft.

Ellis never kissed her as passionately as Jesse did. It was like he was making love to her with his tongue in her mouth. She closed her eyes and enjoyed this moment. He made her panties moist. When he was finished, she panted for air. Jesse left her in a daze. He opened her car door for her. All Aketa could do was stand there.

"I'll see you later," he said.

Aketa just had this look of enjoyment on her face. She was also speechless. She really couldn't believe what she had just experienced. She got into the car. Jesse closed the door. Aketa let down the window.

"See you later," Aketa said.

Aketa drove off.

Chapter 6

Aketa and Jesse have been going out for several months. They enjoy each other's company and have gone to several gatherings. Jesse is trying to show her that he is the man for her.

One night, Aketa let Jesse come over to watch some movies. She had a night plan. Aketa had popped the popcorn and bought wine. She even rented two films, one romantic and one action. She had all of it planned. She even pulled out the blanket just in case.

About an hour later, the doorbell rang. Aketa went to open the door. It was Jesse. He had some roses in his hand.

"These are for you," Jesse said as he handed her roses.

"Thank you," Aketa said. "They're so beautiful."

Aketa let Jesse in. Jesse followed her to the den, where she had everything set up.

"Lovely house," he said.

"Thank you again," Aketa said.

They sat down on the oversized brown leather couch. Jesse put in the action movie first. They both watched it while cuddling up to each other. The suspense got to Aketa. After that movie was over, Aketa put in the romantic film. This is when Jesse started to nibble on her neck. She really couldn't resist it. Then he moved up to her ear. She wanted to push him away, but her other body parts wanted him to keep on going. He whispers in her ear, "I want to make love to you." He started moving his hands down to her designer jeans, which she had put on just for him. As he was kissing her on her neck, he managed to unbutton her pants. He removed them alone with her black lace panties. Then he rose and spread her legs wide open. He was going to dive into this river. She thought that he was going to give it to her with no foreplay. But instead, he started to lick her. He played with her pearl with his tongue. He sucked on it like he was a baby sucking on his mother's breast. Aketa started to moan. Ellis never did this to her. He never bothers to go downtown. Jesse then started to make love to her with his tongue. He stuck his tongue in her like it was his dick. She didn't know how to act. It felt so good to her that she started screaming. She got louder and louder. She couldn't hold it anymore. She hasn't ever had an orgasm like this. She thought that there was something wrong with her.

Jesse licked her up to her nipples. He started sucking on them like he was her baby, trying to get breast milk from them. All Aketa could do was moan. She hasn't moaned like this in years. It felt so good. Then he went up to her neck and sucked it. She moaned even louder. She moaned his name, "Jesse." That is when he decided to give her his all. He went inside her. She spread her legs wide so that he could go deeper inside her. She felt all of him inside her. She didn't want to have another orgasm. She pressed her feet on the couch and started to push back from him. Jesse began to go hard as she tried to run from him. "I don't know why you are running from me," Jesse said. Aketa couldn't hold it any longer. She screamed as she came. He kept on going after she came. All Aketa could do was scream his name from the top of her lungs. Thirty minutes later, Jesse came. He rolled off her and lay next to her, breathing hard. Once he caught his breath, he turned to her.

"Did you enjoy our session?" he asked Aketa.

Aketa couldn't say anything. She was still in shock. She nodded her head yes.

"Do you want to go for round two?" He asked.

Aketa nodded her head yes again.

Jesse started kissing her. He whispered in her ear, "You know that I love you."

Aketa hasn't heard those words in years. She couldn't remember the last time Ellis told her that. It felt good for her to hear that. He kissed her again. And then they went for round two.

Chapter 7

Ellis was at the station. He was sitting at his desk doing some paperwork. Jeremy walked up to the desk.

"Hey," Jeremy said. "What's up?"

"Nothing much," Ellis replied.

"I have something to discuss with you," Jeremy said.

"I am about to grab something to eat," Ellis said. "You can tell me what you want over lunch."

"OK," Jeremy said. "It is on you today."

Ellis got up from his desk. He walked with Jeremy to his car. They drove to The Burger Joint. They both ordered and sat down at one of the tables.

"Now, what did you want to talk to me about?" Ellis asked.

"I wanted to chat to you about this investigation I am doing," Jeremy said. "Well, I was at a restaurant that we are investigating. You know that one that is downtown, Monroe's. The restaurant's owner, Jesse Monroe, is someone I have been investigating for several reasons."

"Do you need to talk to me about it?" Ellis asked.

"When was the last time that you heard from Aketa?" Jeremy asked.

"I picked up the girls from her mother's house. Sometimes I see her, sometimes I don't. I think I haven't talked to her in the last three months. The girl said that she was happy. But she won't let me know where they live. She told the girls not to tell me."

"Do you know that she is dating Jesse Monroe?" Jeremy asked.

Ellis looked shocked. Not his Aketa. He became angry. He became so angry that he balled up his fist. He started biting his bottom lip. Jeremy looked at him and knew he couldn't tell him anything else.

"She leaves me for a criminal," Ellis said.

"Ellis," Jeremy said, "we are still investigating."

"But you all have proof that he is involved in some criminal activities," Ellis said.

"Yes," Jeremy said. "But we are trying to get him on drugs."

"Why drugs?" Ellis asked.

"It is the only thing we can get to stick to him," Jeremy replied.

If it were up to Ellis, he would bust him today. He didn't want a criminal around his family, especially his daughters. Ellis and Jeremy finished their lunch and went back to the station. Ellis was sitting at his desk thinking about what Jeremy had told him. He picked up the office phone and dialed Aketa's cell number. It went to voice mail. He left a message for her to call him ASAP. Ellis sat at his desk for another five minutes. He tried to work but couldn't get his mind off that Aketa was dating someone who was being investigated. So, he called her office.

"Aketa Collin," Diana answered.

"Is Keta in?" Ellis asked.

"May I ask who is calling?" Diana asked.

"Ellis," he replied.

"Oh," Diana said, "Aketa is in a meeting. I will have her call you as soon as she gets out."

"Please tell her to call me ASAP," Ellis said.

"I will," Diana said.

Ellis hung up the phone. He couldn't work thinking about Aketa. He decided to go home.

Chapter 8

Aketa left the office early on Wednesday. Jesse was supposed to meet her at the movies. She wants to see Jesse. Jesse was doing some last-minute paperwork. She knew he was at Monroe's. Aketa decided to go by and surprise him. She hopped in her car and drove to the restaurant.

When she got to Monroe's, there was a whole house. There were people in the lobby waiting to get a table. She saw the hostess at the podium. She didn't look up when Aketa walked up.

"There is an hour's wait," she said without looking to see who it was.

"Is Jesse here?" Aketa asked.

The hostess looked up and saw that it was Aketa. The hostess jumped.

"Oh," she said, "Ms. Collin. I am sorry. He is in the back. Gone on back there."

Aketa walked past the hostess. She went into the restaurant. Several servers stopped and greeted her. They recognized her for being with Jesse. She went through the kitchen. The prep people even spoke to her. Even his sous chef, Caleb, talked to her. She moved toward his office, smiling. It is the happiest she has ever been. She opens the office door to see Jesse and three other men hunched over a table. They all looked back and saw Aketa standing at the door. One of the men moved, and Aketa glanced at what was on the table. Her eyes widened. It was marijuana and crack cocaine. There was a scale on the table with some of the drugs on it.

Jesse saw that it was Aketa. Aketa ran out of the restaurant. Jesse ran after her. He screamed her name. "Aketa!" She didn't look back. Aketa kept running. She ran to the parking lot and hopped in her vehicle very quickly. She locked the doors immediately. Jesse reached out to grab the car door when she took off. Then Jesse jumped into his car and drove fast. He caught up with her at a light. She turned off and went to her house. Jesse was close behind her. She turned into the driveway. He turned in behind her. He rushed out of his car. Aketa jumped out of her vehicle. She dashed to the door. She opened it. Before she could close the door, Jesse had put his foot in the door. He reached out and grabbed her. She stood there shaking. She didn't know what he was going to do.

"I am not going to hurt you," Jesse said.

Aketa stood there still, shaking. She couldn't talk. He was still scaring her.

"Calm down," Jesse said. It is not what you think. I will never harm you. I love you. I would never hurt anyone that I love."

He started to kiss Aketa on the neck. She just stood there and let him do it. He picked her up and carried her to the couch. He then started to pull off her blouse. He unsnapped her bra for her. Aketa let him do it. She was too shocked to stop him. He started sucking on her rather large breasts. She had calmed down and was very aroused. Jesse pulled off her pants. He pulled down his pants and pushed his manhood inside her. As it went inside her, a tear streamed from her eye. More tears streamed down her face as they climaxed together. Jesse pulled up his pants. Aketa lay there motionless. She enjoyed herself but still didn't believe what she had seen. She sat up on the couch. Jesse sat next to her.

"Let me explain myself," he said.

"Explain what?" Aketa asked.

"I used to deal drugs when I was 15 years old. It was something that I did to get money. My family was impoverished. When I was 17, I got busted. I went to jail with my older cousin, Rodney. Rodney was 21. They charged him as an adult. Since it was my first time, the judge let me off on the condition that I make something out of myself. So that was when I went to stay with impoverished parents. I graduated from high school. My granddaddy sent me to culinary school. He watched me walk across the stage. He passed away soon after. By this time, my cousin, Rodney, had escaped prison. He gave me the money to start Monroe's."

"So," Aketa said, "why are the drugs on the table?"

"His warehouse was hot. There are cops all around the warehouse to bust him," said Jesse.

"So, move it out of your restaurant," Aketa said. "They can bust you and send you to prison."

"They are not," he said.

"Do you use drugs?" she asked.

Jesse paused for a minute. He looked at her in her beautiful brown eyes and replied no. Aketa believed him.

"If I ever find out that you are using it," she said, "it is over between us."

"Ok," he said.

Jesse kissed her. He walked to the door and said, "Aketa, you know I love you."

Aketa smiled as she nodded her head yes. Jesse smiled back. He left.

Chapter 9

Aketa looked out the window as Jesse pulled off. That smile she had on her face turned quickly into a frown. Aketa did not want to be with a man that had something to do with drugs. What if the girls were here, she thought to herself? She could have got shot or, worse off, killed.

Aketa went to her bedroom. She stripped out of her clothes. She was in desperate need of a shower. She turned on the hot water in the shower. She got into the shower. She let the water hit every part of her body. She closed her eyes and imagined Ellis was in the shower with her. They used to take showers together before they had the girls. She imagined that water was him touching her. She felt her safest around Ellis.

When she finished washing the scent of Jesse off her, she got out of the shower and returned to her bedroom. She put on her purple nightshirt. She lay in bed. She had thought about what Jesse had done to calm her down. She tried to close her eyes but could only think about Ellis. She was beginning to miss him. But what was the use of returning when he had no intention of marrying her? She loved him, but she wanted more. Jesse said that he wanted more. He provided a life that she was unfamiliar with. He made her do something that she hadn't been able to do in the last five years: climax. She was satisfied with the sex but not with his life.

She fell asleep for about twenty minutes when her phone rang. She reached over for it.

"Hello," she said with a sleepy voice.

"Hey baby," Jesse said. "How are you doing?"

When she heard Jesse's voice, she wanted to hang up but couldn't. She didn't have the strength. He was like a drug to her.

"I'm alright," she responded.

"Do you need anything?" he inquired.

"No," she said softly. "I'm good."

"Are you sure you are alright?" he asked her again.

"I'm good," she answered again.

"If you need anything," Jesse said, "I am just a phone call away."

"Ok," Aketa said.

She hung up the phone and went back to sleep.

Chapter 10

Aketa was in her office. She was working hard as usual. She heard someone arguing outside. She paid it no mind. She thought that it was one of her co-workers arguing over a case. Ellis busted in the door. He was irritated. Aketa looked up and saw that he was in front of her desk.

"May I help you?" Aketa asked.

"Why haven't you called me back?" Ellis inquired angrily.

"I have been busy," she told him.

Diana quickly came in.

"I am sorry," she said. "Mr. Allan stormed past me."

"That's alright," Aketa said. "Mr. Allan was about to take a seat."

"Do you need anything?" Diana asked.

"No," Aketa replied. "That will be all."

Diana walked back out and closed the door behind her. Ellis sat on the couch while Aketa continued to sit at her desk.

"What is so important that you couldn't wait for me to call you back?" Aketa questioned.

"Maybe if you weren't so busy, you would know what I want," Ellis answered.

"Well," she said, "you are here now. Spill it."

"I heard that you are dating again," Ellis said.

"And if I am," Aketa said.

"You don't need to be dating," Ellis said. "You have me."

Aketa laughed and said, "Really? You don't want the same things that I want."

"And what is that?" asked Ellis.

"You don't want a wife," Aketa replied.

"Why ruin a good thing?" he inquired.

"To make it better," she responded.

"I thought what we had was great," he said. "I hope you haven't brought that man around our daughters."

Aketa looked at him. She knew that he knew something.

"And if I did bring another man around them," Aketa said within defense matter.

"I would have to take the girls back to live with me," Ellis said.

"That will never happen," Aketa said.

"You need to keep my girls away from Jesse Monroe," he said.

Aketa looked at him strangely. She never mentioned Jesse's name to him. So, how does Ellis know his name?

"Ok, Sergeant Allan." Aketa said, "How do you know his name?"

Ellis just realized at that moment that he said too much. He didn't mean to let her know what he knew. He also knew that she would think that he was spying on her.

"Just know that Jesse is bad news," Ellis said.

"And how do you know that?" Aketa asked.

Ellis could not tell her that they were investigating Jesse, so he answered, "He was an acquaintance of mine once upon a time."

Aketa looked at him with that eye. She knew he was lying but didn't want to argue with him about it, so she let it go.

"When can I visit with my daughters again?" Ellis inquired.

"This weekend," she answered. "They can spend the whole weekend with you."

"Oh, they can," Ellis said.

"You can pick them up from my mother's house on Friday," she said.

"Ok."

"I will see you then," Aketa said.

"And what is your address again?" Ellis asked.

"None of your business," replied Aketa.

Ellis laughed. He got up and walked out of the office.

Chapter 11

Aketa dropped the girls off at her mother's house. Ellis is supposed to pick them up from there. She told her mother what the deal was between Ellis and her. Aketa kissed the girls goodbye and reminded them not to tell their dad where they lived. Aketa left.

About an hour later, Ellis came to pick up the girls. He was looking around for Aketa. He thought that she would be there, but she was not there.

"Mrs. Collins," Ellis said, "where is Aketa?"

"She had to take care of some business," Mrs. Collins replied.

The girls were sitting in the living room. Their bags were packed with just enough clothes to survive the weekend with their dad. Akera ran to her dad and hugged him. Elisha looked at him.

"I miss you, Daddy," Akera said.

"I miss you too," Ellis told her.

He picked up their bags, put them in the truck, and returned to the house. The girls were standing at the door with their grandma.

"Where do you all stay?" Ellis inquired.

"We stay at," Akera said before Elisha covered her mouth.

"Mama said you can drop us back off at Granny's," Elisha said.

Mrs. Collin gave Akera the evil eye, the look a mama gives you with when you are about to get your tail whipped.

"You can drop them off at my house," Mrs. Collin said.

"Ok," Ellis said.

The girls hugged their grandma. Elisha kissed her on the cheek.

"Behave girls," she told them.

They smiled as they got in the truck with Ellis and waved at their grandma as Ellis pulled off.

Aketa returned to her house to prepare for a movie night with Jesse. She had grabbed a couple of movies that she thought Jesse would be interested in. She also picked up some old-fashioned popcorn that you pop in a skillet. Aketa had cleaned up before the girls left with their father. She wanted it to be a casual night.

About forty minutes later, Jesse was at the door. Aketa answered it. She was delighted to see him. He had brought a picnic basket with food cooked from his restaurant. It mainly was Aketa's favorite, smothered pork chops with dirty rice. He got a bottle of Moscato. As he walked in the door, he kissed her on the cheek. He looked at her and noticed how much she was glowing.

"Why are you smiling so hard?" Aketa asked.

"Because you are glowing," replied Jesse, smiling.

"I am glowing because I am happy," Aketa said. "I am happy that I am with you."

Jesse smiled. He came into the house and set everything up. Aketa went to the kitchen to get utensils. When she came back to the den, Jesse had set up everything. She smelled the pork chops from the kitchen but didn't know that he had dirty rice with them. Aketa was ready to chow down. Before she could take a bite, they prayed over the food. They ate and watched movies.

Chapter 12

Aketa had been working all day long. She had been feeling a little wheezy for the last four days, but she thought it was something that she had eaten. She went to the bathroom when she got to work that day and threw up the breakfast, she had eaten that morning. She cleaned herself up before Diana entered her office with her daily coffee. All day, that same cup of coffee sat on Aketa's desk. She didn't touch it. Diana came into the office. She noticed that Aketa hadn't touched the coffee she had brought her earlier that morning.

"Is there something wrong?" Diana asked.

Aketa looked at Diana strangely and replied, "No, why do you ask?"

"Oh," Diana said.

Diana sat down on the couch. Aketa started getting sick again. She dashed to the bathroom. Diana sat there and waited for her to come out. Aketa cleaned herself up again. She walked over to the couch where Diana was sitting. She was sitting next to her.

"It looks like Jesse, and you have something in the oven," Diana giggled.

"No," Aketa said, "we don't."

"You've been vomiting all day, and you haven't touched your coffee," Diana said. "I would think that you are."

Before Diana could get the words out, Aketa returned to the bathroom. Diana had just gotten off the phone when she came out this time.

"I made you an appointment with Dr. Clemmon," Diana said. "She said she could see you if you came to her office right now."

Aketa got her things together, put on her coat, and got her purse. Then, she went to see Dr. Clemmon.

When Aketa arrived at Dr. Clemmon, she ran to the bathroom and vomited again. She cleaned herself up. She went to the window to check in with the nurse. The nurse gave her some papers to fill out. About twenty minutes later, the nurse called her back. The nurse did her routine, checked vitals, and asked questions. After that, the nurse escorted her to one of the exam rooms. Aketa hates waiting in the exam room. The doctors regularly take too long. Aketa had to use the bathroom. She asked the nurse where the restroom was. She pointed to the restroom and handed her a cup with her name on it.

"Put the cup on the counter when you are finished," she said.

Aketa ran to the restroom, peed into the small cup, and then did what the nurse said. She returned to the exam room, and Dr. Clemmon came in about five minutes later.

"Hello, Ms. Collins," Dr. Clemmons said. "I heard that you have been sick."

Aketa said, "Yes, I have been feeling ill."

"How long have you been feeling this way?" Dr. Clemmon asked.

"About two weeks now," Aketa replied.

"When was your last period?" Dr. Clemmon asked.

"Last month," Aketa answered. "Around about May 8."

Dr. Clemmon looked at her file and said, "Well, your problem is that you are pregnant."

Aketa looked at her in disbelief. After ten years, she will be having another baby.

"You are kidding," Aketa said.

"No," Dr. Clemmon said, "I am not."

"But I am too old to have a baby my age," Aketa said.

"Really, no, you are not," Dr. Clemmon said. "I hope that Ellis takes the news better. Maybe this time it will be a boy."

Aketa didn't want to tell her this was not Ellis's baby. The baby is Jesse's.

"I need blood work on your next visit," Dr. Clemmon said. "By the way, your due date is February 12. In the meantime, we need to take it easy."

Dr. Clemmon gave Aketa some paperwork. Aketa rushed out of the office. She couldn't wait to tell Jesse they would be expecting a baby around Valentine's Day. She drove straight to Jesse's restaurant. When she pulled up, the restaurant wasn't open yet, but Jesse's car was there. She went to the back, where Jesse had told her how to get in. She walked to the back. There was a big black car parked near the door. She opens the door. Aketa walks in. She saw his office door was cracked. She walked to the office door and saw Jesse and his cousin, Rodney, sitting there talking. Just as she was about to open the door, Rodney moved, and she saw some lines of cocaine. She saw Jesse lean in on the desk and snort a line. Aketa was disgusted by what she had seen. Aketa ran out of the restaurant and into her car without Jesse noticing Aketa was there. She got into her vehicle and sat there for a minute. Aketa saw Rodney get into the black car and leave. She didn't want to tell him that she was pregnant. She went home.

Chapter 13

The next day, Aketa went to work late. It is not like her to be late. She is sometimes there before Diana. Diana was sitting at her desk when Aketa walked in. She walked dressed like it was a casual day. She went straight to her office without speaking to Diana. Around noon, Phaedra showed up at the office. Phaedra walks in with three carry-out trays. Aketa was at her desk. As soon as Phaedra walked in, Aketa dashed to the bathroom. When she came out, Phaedra had started to eat. Diana had come in with something for all of them to drink. Aketa sat down at her desk. She cleared herself a spot so that she could enjoy the meal.

"How was your visit to Dr. Clemmons's," Diana asked.

"Diana!" Phaedra shouted. "Let her be the one to bring it up."

"Well," Aketa replied, "I am pregnant."

"What?" Phaedra excellently said.

"I knew it," Diana said. "You are having Jesse's baby."

Aketa frowned when Diana said that. The thought of having Jesse's baby made her nauseating. Phaedra saw the look on her face.

"What's wrong?" Phaedra asked.

"You act as if you are disgusted by the sight of Jesse," Diana said.

Aketa didn't want to tell her friends that she saw her future baby's dad snorting cocaine. They are going to find out sooner or later.

"I caught him doing something he had no business doing," Aketa said.

"You caught him with another woman," Diana said.

Phaedra and Diana leaned in closer to hear what Jesse had done.

"I caught him doing drugs," Aketa said.

Both women looked at her in shock.

"That's it?" Phaedra said. "There is nothing wrong with smoking a little weed. I smoke a little smoke myself."

"It wasn't weed," Aketa said.

"Then what was it?" Diana asked.

"Cocaine," Aketa answered.

"What?" Diana exclaims.

"Yes, cocaine," Aketa said.

"You need to leave that alone," Phaedra said.

"I hope you didn't tell him you were pregnant," Diana said.

"I didn't," Aketa said.

"That's a good thing," Diana said.

"By the way," Aketa said, "I am not taking any phone calls from Mr. Monroe."

"Ok," said Diana.

They finish eating their lunch. Phaedra left.

Later that day, Diana came into Aketa's office. She walked up to her desk. Aketa looked up at her.

"Mr. Monroe has called you about five times since lunch," Diana said. "I think you need to talk to Ellis about this."

Aketa didn't want Ellis to find out about her situation. She knew eventually that she would have to go to him, but Aketa maintained the situation the best way she could.

"I will tell Ellis eventually," Aketa said.

"You don't need Mr. Monroe coming up here acting a fool," Diana said.

Diana walked out. Aketa went back to work.

Chapter 14

It was summertime. Usually, Aketa takes some vacation time and spends it with her girls. Sometimes, she will take them out of town. Other times, they will spend time at the house doing fun things like playing board games. During this vacation, Aketa stayed at home. She didn't feel like going anywhere in her condition. She was playing a board game when the doorbell rang. Elisha was going to answer it, but Aketa told her to stay there. She would answer it. Aketa went to the door. She looked in the peephole. She saw Jesse stand there. She opens the door. She didn't invite him in. Instead, she stepped outside and closed the door. She didn't want him to see the girls.

"Hi, baby," Jesse said.

"What do you want?" Aketa inquired.

"Can I come in and talk to you for a minute?" Jesse asked.

"No, you may not," Aketa reacted.

Jesse knew that there was something wrong.

"And why not?" he asked.

Aketa thought about it for a minute. She knew that she had to tell him something.

"I am sick," she said. "I have the flu."

"The flu," Jesse said.

"Yes," Aketa said, "the flu."

"I can take care of you," Jesse said. "I can make you a hot totty."

"I don't think it's a good idea for you to come in," Aketa said. I'll talk to you later."

"Why don't you want me to come in?" Jesse asked. "Why are you rushing me off? Do you have another man in there?"

"No," Aketa replied, "I don't. Will you please leave?"

"I am not leaving until you let me in," Jesse demanded.

Aketa knew what would scare him and said, "I will call the police."

Jesse's eyes widen. He didn't believe she would call the police, but he didn't want any trouble.

"I'll leave for now," he said. And he left.

Aketa knew right then that she needed to talk to Ellis.

Chapter 15

Aketa had called Ellis. She asked him to meet her at The Burger Joint at noon. She had to discuss it with him but couldn't discuss it on the phone. She felt more comfortable talking about it face-to-face. Ellis became excited. He was so enthusiastic that he arrived at the restaurant an hour early. Ellis sat at the door, waiting for Aketa to walk in. He kept looking at the clock every five minutes. Ellis was so anxious that he had drunk seven cups of coffee before he knew it. He had to go to the restroom. When Ellis came back to his table, Aketa walked in. He looked at her and noticed that she had gotten a little thicker. He thought that it looked cute on her. Ellis rushed back to his table before Aketa noticed. He sat down and waved his hand so Aketa would see him. She saw him and walked toward him. When she got to the table, Ellis stood up to greet her. He went over to her and hugged her. He missed her and the girl so much. He missed her sweet smell. He finally let her go. He pulled out her chair for her. He pushed her to the table. Then he went to take his seat.

"How are you doing?" he asked.

"Just fine," she replied. "How are you?"

"I can't complain," he said. "Are you hungry?"

These days, Aketa is always hungry. It is just like she can't get enough to eat. Ellis called the waiter over to ask Aketa to order. Aketa ordered a cup of water. Two minutes later, the waiter returned with a cup of water for Aketa and another cup of coffee for Ellis.

"So," Ellis said, "what was so important that you couldn't tell me over the phone?"

Aketa didn't know how to tell him, but she had to say something.

"As you already know, "she said, "I am dating Jesse Monroe."

"I know," he said. "You need to leave him alone."

Aketa hated to admit when Ellis was right.

"I hope you haven't brought him around our girls," Ellis said.

"No," Aketa said, "I haven't. I want him to leave me alone."

Ellis's eyes widen. He was waiting for Aketa to tell him what happened.

"I had to stop talking to him," Aketa said. "I even won't accept any of his phone calls. The other day, he showed up to my house."

"He knows where you are staying, but I don't?" Ellis inquired.

Aketa looked at him and kept talking, "I didn't let him in because the girls were there, but he wouldn't leave. He has been calling my job several times a day."

"It sounds like you need to get a restraining order against him," Ellis said. "Why do you want to leave him alone now?"

Aketa took a deep breath and said, "I am pregnant by him."

Ellis put the cup down. He didn't know what else to say. He was mad because Jesse had gotten the love of his life pregnant.

"What are you going to do?" Ellis asked.

"Have the baby and not tell him," Aketa responded.

"I guess you will give me your address now," Ellis said.

Aketa looked down because she didn't want him to know, but he had to know for the girls and her protection.

"7 Vermont Avenue," Aketa said.

"You have been in Rosewood all this time?"

"Yes," Aketa said.

"So, does this mean that we are back together?" Ellis asked.

"We will discuss that later," Aketa retorted.

Their food came. They ate their food. When Aketa was getting ready to go, Ellis walked her to her car. He opens the door for her. Something that he hasn't done for her in years. He gently kissed her on the cheek.

"I will have some of my friends patrol that area," he said. I'll see you later."

He closed Aketa's door. She drove off. He stood there until she turned the corner. He went back to work.

Chapter 16

Jesse had been sending flowers to Aketa's office and house. She has been sending them back to the floral shop, but the load has grown, so she has started throwing them away. Jesse would call her office every hour on the hour. He could no longer call her home or cell phone because she blocked him. She never returned his phone calls. Diana had told him several times not to call back, but he wasn't listening.

Around the second month after Aketa has not talked to Jesse, he shows up at Aketa's office. He waited for Diana to enter her office while she was away from her desk. Diana saw him open the door and dashed over to prevent him from opening it, but it was too late. Aketa was lying on the couch with her feet propped up. This is something that Dr. Clemmon had suggested she do at the office. She had a brief that she was reading. She looked up and saw Jesse standing there. She thought that she was dreaming. She put down the brief and stood up. Jesse stared at her. He couldn't believe what he saw.

"So, this is why you don't want to talk to me," he said.

He walked towards her. He reached out to touch her belly. Aketa moved back. She didn't want him to touch her. She was afraid of him.

"What's wrong?" he asked.

He reached out to her again. Aketa moved back. Diana walked in.

"Is this my baby?" Jesse asked.

Aketa looked at him. He could tell by the way she looked that it was his baby.

"So, you weren't going to tell me that I was going to be a father," Jesse said.

All Aketa could think about was Jesse snorting cocaine. She didn't want her baby around that, father or not.

"You need to leave," Aketa said.

"I want to be there for you and the baby," Jesse said.

"Will you please leave?" Aketa asked him again.

"You are just being moody," Jesse said.

Aketa banged up her fist. She wanted to hit him, but she didn't.

"You need to leave now!" Aketa shouted.

"Do you need me to call security?" Diana asked.

"That's alright," Jesse said.

Jesse walked out of the office. He was furious. Aketa sat back down on the couch. Diana sat next to her.

"Are you alright?" Diana asked. "Do I need to call Ellis?"

"Yes," Aketa replied. "You don't have to call Ellis. I'll be alright."

"Ok," Diana said.

Diana got up and went back to her desk. Aketa picked up her brief and started reading again.

Later that day, Diana and Aketa were getting ready to wrap up their day. They walked out together. When Aketa got to her car, she saw the word bitch written on it. All four of her tires were slashed.

"You need to call Ellis," Diana said.

Aketa called Ellis. Ten minutes later, he came with his cop friend, Demetrius. Demetrius examined the car.

"Are you alright?" Ellis inquired.

"I'm ok," she replied.

She told Ellis what had happened earlier in the office. She spoke about how he found out she was pregnant and said she wanted to do it for the baby and her.

"I am moving in with you," he said.

"Why," Aketa asked.

"I don't think this is the last time we will hear from Jesse," Ellis said. "And to make sure nothing else happens."

Aketa didn't want Ellis to live with them again. She had adjusted to life without him, but the girls would be glad he moved back in. She will feel a lot safer with him around.

"Ok," Aketa said.

Diana looked at her in shock. She looked at Aketa. Aketa smiled. Then Diana thought about it and knew it was for her safety.

The tow truck came to take Aketa's car to the shop.

"I'm taking you home," Ellis said.

He opened his car door for her to get in. He got into the squad car, and Demetrius got in soon after. They took Aketa home.

Chapter 17

A week later, Ellis moved in with Aketa and the girls. The girls were thrilled that their dad was living with them again. This meant that they no longer had to stay with their grandmother. Aketa felt safe with him around. He moved his things into the guest room, but Aketa wasn't going to allow him to sleep back with her.

A week had passed since Ellis moved in with Aketa. Ellis was off. The girls were at school, and Aketa drove his truck to work. He was sitting in the den looking at an old cop show on TV. He was still in his pajamas when the doorbell rang. Ellis got up to answer the door. He opens the door to see a bronze man standing before him. He was dressed in a baby blue polo shirt and khaki pants. He had flowers in his hand. He looked up and saw Ellis standing at the door.

"May I help you," Ellis said.

"Is Aketa here?" Jesse asked.

"No, she isn't," Ellis replied. "Who are you?"

Jesse smiled and said, "I am her baby daddy."

Ellis giggled and said, "The last time I checked, she only had one baby daddy, me."

Jesse stopped smiling. He became furious.

"I am her only baby daddy," Jesse angrily said.

"Well," Ellis said, "we have two beautiful daughters together. She would have mentioned it to me if she had had another baby daddy."

Jesse looked at him, surprised. He didn't know that she had two daughters. They have been dating for a year, and she never introduced him to her family.

"Well," Jesse said, "she is having my baby now. May it will be a boy."

"She doesn't want anything to do with you," Ellis said.

"She will soon," Jesse said.

"No, she doesn't want you," Ellis said, "and you need to leave."

"Tell her I came by," Jesse said.

Jesse walked off. Ellis slams the door. He went to get his phone and called Aketa.

"Hello," Aketa said.

"How are you doing?" Ellis asked.

"Fine," she answered. "I haven't had any morning sickness."

"That's good," he said. "You had a visitor to stop by the house."

"Who was it?" she inquired.

"That punk ass bastard," Ellis said.

Aketa went into silence. She didn't say anything for a while.

"Are you still there?" Ellis asked.

"Yes," Aketa said.

"You need to go down to the courthouse and file a restrain order against his crazy ass before I have to kill this ignorant bastard," Ellis said.

"I will," Aketa said.

"I will talk to you when you get to the house this evening," Ellis said.

"Ok, bye," Aketa said.

She put down her cell phone and picked up the office phone. Diana picked up the other line.

"Get Judge Brown on the phone," she said.

"May I ask why," Diana asked.

"No, you may not," she said.

"Ok," Diana said.

She called Judge Brown for Aketa. She buzzed Aketa when she was on the line.

"Hello," she said.

"Hello, Judith," Aketa said. "This is Aketa Collin."

"I know who this is," Judge Brown said. "What's going on?"

"I need a favor," Aketa said.

"What is it," Judge Brown asked.

"I need a restraining order against someone," Aketa replied.

"Who?"

"Jesse Monroe," Aketa answered.

"Not Chef Jesse Monroe of Monroe's," Judge Brown said. "I love his food. What did he do to you?"

"Stalking me," Aketa answered.

"Do Ellis know about this?" the judge inquired.

"Yes," responded Aketa, "he is the one that told me to go file a restraining order."

"I am surprised he didn't try to kill him," the judge stated. "Send me over the paperwork, and I will sign it."

"Thank you, Judith," Aketa said.

Aketa hung up the phone. She felt a sigh of relief. Maybe now he will leave me alone, Aketa thought to herself. She went back to work.

Chapter 18

The last five weeks have been hell for Aketa. She has had all her windows broken out of the car several times. All the security cameras caught were someone dressed in all black, but they never could get a close enough look at him. Ellis started to take her to and from work. He also took the girls to and from school. This routine was working out fine.

A few weeks later, Mr. Wilson called Aketa into his office. She went in, not knowing what was going on. She opened the door of Mr. Wilson's office and walked in. Mr. Wilson looked up and saw Aketa standing in his office.

"Hello, Ms. Collin," he greeted her. "You can have a seat."

She sat in one of Mr. Wilson's big chairs in front of his desk.

"I meant to talk to you earlier," he said. Has everything been going alright?"

"Everything is fine, Mr. Wilson."

"Well," Mr. Wilson said, "I received an anonymous phone call from a client saying some very unethical things about you."

"Excuse me," Aketa said. She scooted to the edge of her seat.

"He said that you have had sex with him on serval occasions, and you took money from him," Mr. Wilson told Aketa.

Aketa knew it wasn't anyone but Jesse. She was concerned that her boss would fire her because of what Jesse said. He wasn't her client but could destroy her reputation as an attorney. A cokehead damaged something that she had worked so hard on. She was drained of everything Jesse had done since he found out she wanted nothing to do with him. She looked down because she was ashamed that Jesse had dragged her job into this.

"Ms. Collin," Mr. Wilson said, "are you alright?"

She paused for a minute and answered, "Yes, sir."

"Well," Mr. Wilson said, "I don't believe a word he said."

Aketa looked up at Mr. Wilson.

"I believe someone is out to get you," Mr. Wilson said. "It would be a good idea for you to take some time off and rest. Jones can work on your case while you are away. You can get some rest. You are carrying a little one."

"Thank you, Mr. Wilson," Aketa said.

They both rose out of their seats. Mr. Wilson walked over and shook Aketa's hand.

"You take it easy," Mr. Wilson said.

"I will," Aketa said.

Aketa went to her office. Diana walked in behind her. She wanted to know what Mr. Wilson talked to Aketa about. Diana sat on the couch.

"Well," Diana said, "What did he say?"

Aketa sat at her desk in silence. She was still trying to process Jesse's threat to get her fired.

"You got fired?" Diana inquired.

Aketa looked at her and replied, "No."

"Then what happens?" Diana asked.

"Jesse has been calling to complain to Mr. Wilson about my ethics," Aketa replied.

"He did what!"

Before Aketa could answer, a delivery boy brought food from Jesse's restaurant. Aketa looked at the boy in shock.

"Mr. Monroe sent this over," the boy said.

"You can take it back to him," Diana said.

"Mr. Monroe said don't bring it back," the boy said. "He cooked it himself."

"You can have it," Aketa said. "I wouldn't eat anything that bastard cooks."

"I wouldn't eat it either," the boy said.

He winked as he said his last statement. Aketa and Diana looked at him strangely. Then Aketa thought about it. Jesse had poisoned the food. Aketa called the police. The police came, and a report was made. The police went over to Monroe's and arrested Jesse. He had violated the restraining order that Aketa had against him.

Chapter 19

Two weeks later, Aketa went back to work. She is a little bit better. She needed the rest. She felt more comfortable returning to work since Jesse had been locked up. She even told Ellis that she wanted to drive herself to work. She walked into the building, and everyone was happy to see her. She walked by Diana's desk. Diana stood up to hug Aketa. She was glad that she was back.

"I am glad that you are back," Diana said.

"I am too," Aketa said.

Aketa went into her office and went to work. Ellis would call her every two hours to ensure she was alright. He also brought her lunch.

On Wednesday, Aketa went to work as usual. At lunchtime, Ellis brought Aketa lunch. He had brought her favorite, Mexican. Ellis set her lunch on the mahogany coffee table. Aketa got up from her desk and went to sit on the couch. She smiled at Ellis.

"Thank you so much," Aketa said as she started to eat.

"You're welcome," Ellis replied.

"Do you want some?" she inquired.

"No, thank you," Ellis said. "I need you to come straight home tonight."

"Why?" Aketa inquired.

"Just come straight home," Ellis demanded.

"Ok," Aketa said.

Ellis kissed her on the forehead. Then he left.

About an hour later, Diana received a phone call from her daughter's school and entered the office.

"Excuse," she said.

Aketa looked up at Diana.

"I have to leave early today," Diana told Aketa. "Mya is sick."

"I hope that she gets better," Aketa said.

"Thank you," Diana said. "I will see you tomorrow."

"Stay at home and take care of Mya," Aketa said. "I can manage on my own for a day or two."

"OK," Diana said. "I will call and let you know how we are doing."

Diana left for the day.

Later that day, Aketa just wrapped up for the day. She cleaned off her desk. She picked up her briefcase. She grabbed her jacket and walked out the door. She felt she was being followed as she walked into the parking garage.

She looked behind her. She saw nothing. She continued to walk to her car when her phone rang.

"Hello," she said as she answered the phone.

"Hi, Honey," Ellis said. "Are you on your way home?"

"Yes," Aketa replied.

"How far are you from the house?" he asked.

"I just got to my car," she replied.

"OK," he said. "I will see you when you get here."

"Bye," Aketa said.

As soon as she hung up the phone, someone ran behind her. Before she could scream, Jesse put a handkerchief over her nose and mouth. She passed out.

Chapter 20

It has been three hours since Ellis spoke to Aketa. He thought that she would be at home by now. Earlier, Ellis had ensured the girls did their homework and dropped them off at their grandmother's house. He even cooked dinner for Aketa. He wanted everything to be perfect. He had the table set up for a romantic dinner for two. He sat on the couch, waiting for Aketa to open the door. He went into his pocket and pulled out a ring box. He opens the box to look at the two karts he just purchased for her. He has the intention of proposing to her. He pulls out his phone and calls her. All he got was her answering service. Then he called Diana.

"Hello," she said.

"Hi, Diana," Ellis said.

"Hi, Ellis," she said. "What's up?"

"Do you know where Keta is?" he asked.

"I haven't seen her since earlier," Diana said. "I had to leave early because Mya was sick."

"Thanks, Diana," Ellis said.

"You're welcome," Diana said.

Ellis hit the end button. He grabbed his keys. Ellis went to his truck. Before he took off, he called his homeboy, Demetrius, to meet him at Aketa's job. He went to Aketa's job. He saw her car in her parking place. Soon after he pulled up, Demetrius pulled up. Ellis got out of his truck. He looked around her car. He saw her ground near the driver's door. Demetrius got out of his car and walked over to Ellis.

"I found her keys," Ellis said. "I think that sorry son of a bitch kidnapped her."

"Did she have her phone on her?" Demetrius asked

Ellis opened the car and looked in it. He did not see her phone or her briefcase, so he called the phone.

"I am going to call Jeremy to trace it," Demetrius said.

Demetrius called Jeremy. Jeremy traced the phone to a warehouse on the outskirts of Butler. Demetrius and Ellis drove to the warehouse, and Jeremy met them there. They saw Jesse's car parked near the building. Jeremy exited his vehicle and entered the truck with Ellis and Demetrius.

"What are we going to do?" Jeremy asked.

"We are going to wait for backup," Demetrius replied.

"You are so by the book," Jeremy said.

Before they could say anything to Ellis, he ran out of the truck toward the building. Demetrius and Jeremy ran after him. They didn't know what they were getting into. They didn't want anyone to get hurt, especially Aketa. They finally caught up with Ellis at the warehouse. He was about to open the door when Jeremy grabbed him.

"Wait a minute," Jeremy said, "we don't know what we are getting into."

Ellis looked at Jeremy and Demetrius, deranged. They knew they couldn't stop him, so Ellis entered the warehouse.

Chapter 21

Aketa woke up handcuffed to a chair. She looked around and noticed that she was in the place where Jesse had their first date. She looked up and saw Jesse walking up to her. She was scared. She didn't know what he might do to her.

"Hello, Sweetie," he said to her. "I hope you and our son are doing fine."

He kissed her on the cheek, and she pulled away. She touched her belly. He felt the baby kick. He smiled.

"My boy is strong," he said. "Are you hungry?"

"Why would I eat anything from you?" Aketa asked.

"It's alright," he replied. "I didn't poison the food this time."

"So, you admit that you sent me poison food to kill baby and me," Aketa said.

"I didn't admit to anything," Jesse said. "I am just trying to care for you and my boy."

Aketa tried to get loose.

"There's no way that you are getting out of that chair without the key," Jesse said.

Jesse dangled the keys in her face. Aketa stopped trying to get loose. Jesse went over to the table and picked up the plate. He walked over towards her. He took a spoonful of sweet potatoes. Aketa tightens her lips.

"Come on," Jesse said, "eat something for Daddy."

Aketa turned her head away from him. He held the spoon to the side of her head.

"You got to eat something," Jesse said. "You are carrying my boy."

Ellis was in the warehouse. He heard Jesse talking. He just followed Jesse's voice to where Jesse had Aketa. She was in a chair restrained from moving. He saw her turning her head, and he lost it. He ran towards Jesse. Before Jesse knew it, he was on the floor with food on him. Jesse looked up and was shocked to see it was Ellis. Ellis was punching him. Jeremy and Demetrius ran in to see Ellis beating Jesse. As Demetrius ran and tried to pry Ellis off Jesse, Ellis got off Jesse and pulled his gun out. Jesse lay there scared. Jeremy ran over to the chair to which Aketa was handcuffed and took them off of her.

"Don't do it!" Aketa shouted.

"No," Ellis shouted, "He deserves it!"

"Back down, man," Jeremy said.

"Why?" Ellis asked. "This bastard hurt my wife."

Everyone looked at Ellis in shock. They have never heard him call Aketa his wife.

"He is not worth it, man," Demetrius said.

Ellis stared at Jesse. He gave Jesse that stare as if he was going to kill him at any given moment. Jesse was looking at frightening.

"Don't pull the trigger," Aketa cried. "Please put the gun down."

Ellis continues to stare at Jesse. In his mind, he wanted to pull the trigger. But he knew he wouldn't be any better than him if he did that. He put down the gun. Demetrius went to get the gun. Jesse got up off the floor.

"She is still pregnant with my baby," Jesse said.

Ellis ran to him and sucker-punched him back to the ground. Jeremy grabbed Ellis before he could throw another punch.

"If I ever see you around my family again," Ellis said, "I will kill you."

Demetrius handcuffed Jesse. Soon after, the police arrived. Ellis walked over to Aketa. He helped her up out of the chair.

"Are you alright," Ellis inquired.

"Yes," she replied.

Ellis kissed her. Aketa didn't resist. She was happy that her man came to her rescue. He stopped kissing her and got down on one knee. He reached into his pocket and pulled out a ring.

"Aketa Renee Collin," he said, "will you marry me?"

Aketa started crying. The moment she has been waiting for is happening now.

"Yes," she replied.

Ellis put a two-kart princess-cut diamond ring on her finger.

"Baby, this is my investment in our future together, "he said. "I will never let you go again."

He got up, and they kissed passionately.

Chapter 22

One year later, Aketa is in her room. Her friends, Phaedra and Diana, were in the room with her. Both were wearing long chiffon dresses with rhinestone straps. Phaedra was wearing the red version. Diana was wearing an ivory one. Elisha was wearing the junior version of the dress, which was pink. Akera sat by the wagon, playing with Elisha and Ellis, Jr. Aketa was at her vanity smiling. Her mother was in the room helping her prepare for her big day. Mrs. Collins helped Aketa put on her mantilla veil.

"Are you ready?" her mother asked.

"I have been ready for the last sixteen years," Aketa answered.

"Before you get married," Phaedra said, "I want us to pray."

They joined hands, and Phaedra started to pray.

"Lord," Phaedra started, "we want you to bless this couple on this day. We want to pray for their union. Let them know what you have united no man can break apart. God, we ask that you let them know you will see them through the good and bad times. You will keep them up in your holly arms. God strengthen their kids. Let them grow up to see that they, too, can have the same type of love their parents have for each other. We know that everything happens in your timing. You have had this union in the works for the last 16 years. And know that they will be together until the end of time. In Jesus name, we pray, amen."

Then, there was a knock on the door. Diana went to answer it. It was Demetrius. He told her that it was time. They each got their bouquets and lined up outside.

The wedding was outside in the backyard of their house. It was filled with red, pink, and ivory roses. As the music began, Ellis came out with Jeremy and Demetrius. They stood at the altar with Judge Brown, who officiated the wedding. The first person to come down the aisle was Elisha. After she was Diana. The last maid was the maid of honor, Phaedra. They each were carrying three roses. When Phaedra reached the altar, Akera came out tossing rose petals and pulling EJ in a red wagon. EJ had the rings on a red pillow. When they reached the end of the aisle, *Back at One* by Brian McKnight started to play. Everyone stood up as Aketa entered the garden. She wore a wore a long ivory mermaid-style dress. The top was embossed in pearl and rhinestones. The bottom flared out like a fin. The back had a short train. Her veil was made of Italian lace over her face. Ellis saw Aketa, and tears began to stream down his face. She was so beautiful to him. Aketa was escorted in by her mother, Mrs. Collins. She wore a red dress with a pink rose on the collar. Mrs. Collins pulled back her Aketa's veil when they were at the altar. She kissed her on the cheek and went to take her seat. Ellis and Aketa faced each other.

Judge Brown begins the ceremony by saying. "Dearly beloved. Today, we gathered to unite Ellis Cardan Allan with Aketa Renee Collin. If anyone objects to this union, speak now or forever, and hold your peace."

Everyone looked around the room to see if anyone objected to this union. After a minute, it was determined that nobody objected.

"Ellis and Aketa decide to write their vows," Judge Brown stated.

Ellis says, "In the past sixteen years, God has blessed me with many things. He blessed me with three beautiful kids and a job I love. But most of all, God blessed me with a woman that always has my back. God blessed me with you. I knew from day one that you would be my one and only. I knew that God sent you to me. I love you, Aketa. Always and forever."

Then Aketa said her vows, "I met you on the first day of my college life. You were the first person that I met.

I knew right then and there that we would be together. I started imagining you with me. I invested my all into you. Even when we were apart, I never stopped loving you. You were always on my mind. You are my protector and the father of my kids. I love you always and forever. I thank God for allowing me to be your Proverb 31."

Judge Brown said, "I now pronounce you husband and wife. You may kiss your bride."

Ellis leaned to kiss Aketa. Before he kissed her, he whispered in her ear, "Thank you for investing in me."

Epilogue

It has been six years since Jessie set foot outside of Fort Newton Correctional Faculty. He pleaded guilty to false imprisonment. The judge sentenced him to fifteen years of prison with the possibility of parole in eleven years. As they were taking him back to the holding cell, he looked back to see if Aketa was sitting at the back of the court. Instead, he saw Ellis with his cop friends smiling about the sentence. Jessie just wished he could have seen Aketa just one more time before they locked him up. He never saw their son. She had him while Jessie was in jail waiting for trial. He also heard about Aketa's marriage to Ellis. "It should have been me," he thought to himself every day since he had been locked up.

Part of Jessie's plea deal is that he has no contact with Aketa or his son. He never saw his son, nor did he know his name. He just called him Junior because that is what he would have named him. He would lay in his bunk and think of all the things he would have done with him. By now, he would have been teaching how to slide into home plate after knocking the ball out of the park. Jessie never saw his son's first steps. He wanted to be in his son's life but couldn't because of his mother.

Jesse thought that he should have taken her to Vegas and married her while he could. But she saw his true colors. Aketa saw him doing drugs. She saw him dealing with people that didn't mean him any good. Aketa was his dream woman. She was the woman that he had been looking for his whole life, and he let her slip out of his hand. But he couldn't blame anyone but himself. If it wasn't for his actions, Aketa would have been Mrs. Jesse Monroe.

As he lay there thinking, a prisoner stopped by his cell. He was pushing the library cart full of books.

"Hey man," he said in his deep, smooth voice. "Do you want to read today's newspaper?"

Jesse got out of his bunk and walked over to the door of the cell. The young man handed him a newspaper and walked off. Jessie went back to his bunk and sat on it. When the paper opened to read it, a brown envelope fell out onto the floor. He picks it up and opens it. The first thing he pulled out was some pictures. He looked at the first picture, which featured a little boy who resembled himself. He was wearing a baseball uniform and holding a baseball bat. Jessie frowned as he read the back of the picture. It read Ellis, Jr. 5. He looked through the rest of the pictures. After the last picture, there was a letter. It was from his cousin Rodney. Since he was in prison, he couldn't have any communication with Rodney because of his parole conditions. He had to find someone on the inside to look for a letter to his cousin. Jesse started to read the letter.

What's up, Man,

I know it has been a while, but you know the deal. I couldn't write to you directly because you know I am still on parole. I will be getting off of this bull shit in the next six months. After six months, I will be able to write to you directly, but this will take some time.

I hope that you are doing well. I know that you love that bitch, Aketa. You know she married that cop who arrested you. They named that baby after him. He thinks that the cop is his dad. That is fucked up. If he wasn't a cop, I would have him killed. You remember my baby mama, Kalonda. Well, our daughter, Layla, goes to school with one of Aketa's girls. They are good friends. She often visits their house. She spent the night there just the other night. That is how I was able to get pictures of the boy.

Even though you think that everyone turned your back on you, I haven't. I will be there for you just like you were there for me during my dark times. Whatever you need, I got you. Just let a brother know. In the meantime, keep your head up.

Rodney

Jesse put the letter back in the envelope. He lay in his bunk looking at the picture of his son. "One day, you are going to find out who is your real daddy," he mumbled to himself.

Two years later, the Collins family gathered in the backyard, decorated with blue and green streamers, balloons, and a big banner that read "Happy 8th Birthday, Ellis, Jr!" Laughter filled the air as Junior's friends chased each other around, and the smell of hot dogs and burgers on the barbecue grill drifted in the air. His sisters wore T-shirts that read "Happy Birthday, Junior." They watched as their little brother ran happily around the backyard. Ellis was on the grill, making sure the food did not burn. Aketa was organizing the gift table. As she moved around the gifts, she saw a red and white superhero-wrapped box with a card on it. The envelope read To Junior From Daddy. Aketa and Ellis went together and bought Junior a gift. This gift came as a surprise. Aketa didn't think too much about it because she thought Ellis might have bought him something else.

After everyone sang "Happy Birthday" to Junior, everyone ate. Then, it was time to open the gifts. Junior picked up the red-and-white-wrapped box. Junior beamed with excitement as he tore into gifts, his friends clapping around him.

Aketa whispered into Ellis's ear, "I thought that we agreed to buy Junior one gift."

Ellis turned to look at Aketa and said, "I didn't buy him anything extra."

Junior saw the envelope and opened it. A fifty-dollar bill dropped out of the card. Before Junior could read the card, Ellis walked up to him and took the card out of his hand. He also swooped down and picked up the fifty-dollar bill before Junior realized what it was.

"I'll take care of this," Ellis said.

Ellis walked back over to Aketa. He gave her the envelope with the card. Junior didn't care because he was happy that the gift was a remote-control car. Aketa read the card.

I hope that you enjoy your birthday gift. Daddy will be seeing you soon.

Love your real dad,

Jesse

www.ingramcontent.com/pod-product-compliance
Lightning Source LLC
Chambersburg PA
CBHW050423110726
47899CB00008B/2834